Celeste

A Kay Melbrell Novella

Kay Melbrell

KAY MELBRELL BOOKS

Book Cover Illustration by Jessica Parker

1st edition 2024

To Susan

one of my greatest supporters

Contents

Indentured

Prologue

Laughter and the clinking of dinnerware were familiar, comfortable sounds to Gregory. He sat back and sipped on his sweet summer wine as he enjoyed the stories his sisters told from their apprenticeships.

A loud banging on the door of their modest home cut through the merriment, startling those at the table. Gregory's mother and two sisters looked to him with puzzlement furrowing their brows.

"Who could be calling in such a manner at this hour?" one of his sisters asked. Gregory wiped his mouth on his napkin and excused himself, but before he could take two steps toward the door, it burst open. Three mudmen—constables who wore crisp deep brown uniforms and tended to do the dirty work of those that could afford it—burst through the door.

Two of them pushed past Gregory as the third—with three silver pins on his collar—stood in the doorway and read from a thick piece of paper, "All members of the Heptain household are hereby detained and their material possessions forfeit to the office of the magistrate pending the resolution of a collection complaint."

Emmaline, his youngest sister, screamed when one of the mudmen grabbed her by the arm. Gregory shouted in protest and received a knock to his knees from a billystick, the hard lacquered club sweeping his legs out from underneath him. He and his family were quickly restrained and thrown in the back of an enclosed wagon, the click of the lock deepening the fear running through him.

His sisters frightened sobs filled the small space as Gregory checked on his mother. The mudmen had banged her around when they shoved her in the wagon, and she was dabbing a small wound on her forehead with a handkerchief. Gregory took the small, lacey piece of fabric from her and tried to examine the cut, but the single barred window in the door let in too little of the light from the street lamps.

Standing, he looked out the window. The mudmen were piling their family possessions into another wagon. Gregory slammed his palm against the door and shouted, "What is the meaning of this? How dare you attack us in our own home!"

One of the mudmen banged his billystick against the bars. "Shut it! You'll get your say soon enough."

Gregory's mother tugged at his pant leg. "Sit down, Gregory. You'll only agitate them more. Help me settle your sisters. We'll be in front of the magistrate soon enough." He nodded and settled in between his frightened sisters, wrapping an arm around each one's shoulders and holding them close. They stopped crying but their bodies were still stiff with worry.

While they waited for the mudmen to finish loading all their belongings, Gregory's mind wandered to the last time the constabulary intruded on his life. He had been young when his father's back-alley gambling dragged the family in front of a magistrate, but that experience, while intense, had not been as intrusive as this.

Loud arguing outside their home with mudmen had been followed by rough handling into an open wagon. After which they had stood in front of a man in black robes who delivered stern words to his father. When they returned home, his father and mother had an explosive argument—one that left him comforting his little sisters much as he was now. That had been the last time Gregory saw his father.

After waiting for what must have been an hour, the prison wagon jerked into motion and Gregory, his sisters, and their mother endured a bumpy ride to the magistrate hall. Upon their arrival, the door opened, and mudmen grabbed Gregory's mother, yanking her out and onto her feet. Gregory began to protest, but was silenced with a threatening wave of a billystick. Placing himself between the mudmen and his sisters, he helped them out as well as he could.

The judgment room was the same as in his memory. A man in black robes with long gray hair and a thin face sat at a large oak table, which stood upon a raised platform. Three witnesses sat in lightly upholstered chairs at a narrow table in front of the platform. A wooden cell stood on the left for the accused to wait their turn, but being this late, it was empty. Finally, two tables stood in front of the platform, one for the party filing the complaint and one for the poor soul defending against it.

This evening, a bear of a man in a fancy suit sat at the one on the right, a stack of papers neatly gathered in front of him. He turned when Gregory's group was brought into the room and sized them all up, his gaze lingering on Gregory the longest.

"What is the meaning of this?" Gregory protested, trying to wrench his arm from the mudman's iron grip.

The magistrate pointed a bony finger at Gregory. "Do not speak unless spoken to, boy." He turned to the man sitting at the table. "Now that all the concerned parties are present, let's begin. Who represents the next of kin to one Thaddeous Gregory Heptain?"

Finally extricating himself from the mudman's grasp, Gregory stepped forward with his heart in his stomach. It had been sixteen years since he last heard his father's name. "I do. I speak for the Heptain household."

"State your name for the witnesses."

"Gregory James Heptain." The witnesses marked on documents in front of them then nodded to the magistrate, who waved his hand toward the mudmen holding Gregory's family. The mudmen roughly lowered the family into the chairs at the defendant's table before standing by the door.

"And who represents the party of the complainant?" The magistrate balanced thin round spectacles near the tip of his nose and picked up a document.

"Trenton Baske, Your Honor," the large man at the other table said as he stood, his big voice matching his size.

After receiving another nod from the witnesses, the magistrate said, "Let it be known that Mr. Baske has executed his right to collection from the kin line of a deceased debtor to which Mr. Baske was owed the adjusted sum of 300,000 sovereign ducats..."

The rest of the magistrate's words faded to a buzz as the news settled over Gregory. Not only was this the first he had heard of his estranged father's death, but the sheer size of the debt was staggering.

Baske's voice broke through Gregory's stupor. "Yes, Your Honor, I exert my right to transfer the debt to the next of kin as well as my right to immediate repayment."

"You're crazy. I don't have that much money. Also, I haven't seen nor heard from my father in over a decade. Why must I be burdened with his debt?" Gregory felt like he was drowning.

"That's a 10 ducat fine for speaking out of turn," The magistrate said, making a note on one of his papers, with the witnesses echoing his actions. Gregory moved to speak again, but his mother put a hand on his arm. He looked into her knowing eyes and he stayed his tongue.

"What assets do you have to put against this debt, Mr. Heptain?" The magistrate spoke with an impartial tone, but Gregory saw the furtive knowing glances that passed between the official and Baske.

"I decline to accept this burden." Gregory, his mother, and his sisters had a comfortable life, but their holdings paled in comparison to what was being asked of them.

Baske chuckled softly as the magistrate flashed his teeth in a menacing smile. "Your defense is rejected. Mr. Baske is well within his rights to initiate this proceeding and have it approved in his favor." He folded his hands on top of his papers and locked eyes with Baske. "Let it be known that the kin of Thaddeous Gregory Heptain are hereby ordered to assume his debt. Their material possessions are to be seized and evaluated, to which the marketable value will be applied to the debt. His wife and children are hereby indentured to Mr. Baske's farm or other business holdings, as he sees fit, for the period of time that reasonable wages would pay off the sum owed."

The women gasped. "No," Gregory shouted. "No, please. Take me. Just me. I'm young and of strong mind and body. I will take on this burden alone. Leave them out of this."

"30 ducats for the outburst. Mr. Baske?" The magistrate raised an eyebrow.

Trenton Baske made a show of looking up and down each person at the defendant's table. "I agree to defer my right to indenture all of the late Heptain's kin, pending an evaluation of the young man's ability to repay the debt through labor. I'm not heartless. I have a daughter of my own, and I wouldn't want her wallowing in pig slop if I could help it."

Though the record that the witnesses scribed would later read as Baske showing mercy, the threat held within his tone echoed inside of Gregory. He embraced each member of his family, tears streaming down their faces with promises on their lips to provide as much of their modest salaries as they could to help pay down the debt. Gregory kissed each on their forehead and told them not to worry, though his stomach was twisting into knots. The rough hands of mudmen hauled him out of the judgement room and loaded him into a wagon that would take him, along with half a dozen other newly indentured men, to the Baske farm.

***

Gregory struggled to push the triangular blade through the hard compacted earth. His whole body ached.

As they had arrived at the sprawling operation in the early morning hours, a sinewy man shoved a tool into some of the newly indentured men's hands and sent them to other task masters. Gregory was ushered past outbuildings, animal pens, and more on his way to fallow fields. An iron plow was provided, and as he had been immediately set to work.

Slumping against the plow to catch his breath, he wiped his face of sweat and dirt with his sleeve, then let his gaze wander to where the edges of the farm met a shady forest. The words from the overseer about the financial and physical consequences for leaving the farm echoed in his mind. Though he tried to ignore the tugging he felt within his core, a desire to step into the woods beyond the fields built. When a bell sounded, marking the end of the day's work, Gregory found himself walking into the forest, his body exhausted and the blisters on his hands weeping.

Just as the sun kissed the tops of the trees, Gregory entered a secluded hollow. On the opposite end, a waterfall flowed into a serene pool, which reflected the fiery oranges and pinks of the sunset. Tension started to melt from his shoulders as he made his way to the water, and kneeling at its edge, Gregory gingerly lowered his hands into it. They were raw, covered in ulcerations, and looked as angry as he felt, but the water was soothing and eased his pain. As the moment stretched, he closed his eyes, letting the water take some of his frustrations. He sat there in the quiet stillness and let tears slip silently down his dirty face, his internal pain clashing with the mystical tranquility of this place.

Small noises brought his attention above him, and he watched colorful wrens flit between the branches of the canopy that arched overhead. Almost wishing he never had to leave this place, Gregory sighed as fireflies started to twinkle around him. Being out of bounds was dangerous enough, but missing a bed check would compound his already impossible troubles. He removed his hands from the water and inspected them, furrowing his brow. They looked to have fewer blisters. Maybe his internal turmoil had made them seem worse than they were?

Deciding to ignore the incongruity, Gregory wiped his hands on his clothes and hurried from the glade. While content with his choice to break the rules and come to this peaceful place, he was not interested in finding out how truthful the overseer had been with his colorful descriptions of consequences.

Entering the farm feeling lighter than before, he wondered why his clothes were damp and where the time had gone. He looked behind him at the woods that lined the northern boundary of the fields, and something inside tugged at him. A sense of something important danced just outside the grasp of his thoughts as he slipped into his assigned longhouse.

Just in time for bed checks.

1

Cornered

Gregory watched the stone skip across the crystal-clear pool as a fine spray from the nearby waterfall floated over him. The refreshing tingle of the mist mingled with the relaxing beauty of the sunset, and eased his sore muscles. How quickly his life had gone from carefree to complicated. Three months ago, he was tending a general store during the day and laughing with his sisters and his mother over family meals in the evenings. His dreams had been simple: to earn enough to buy that general store, have a family, and pass the store down to his children. But now?

Picking up a new handful of smooth, flat rocks, he contemplated the sudden shift in his circumstances. An ordinary night had turned into something life changing with those mudmen breaking down the door and dragging him in front of the slick-haired magistrate.

Not only did Gregory learn of his estranged father's passing, but he was also informed that a nearby farm baron, Trenton Baske, had bought his father's back-alley gambling debt. Gregory's father had worked on the farm for three years before his passing, but still his balance remained largely intact. Trenton had scoured local birth and marriage records to find his dead debtor's next of kin.

Gregory's entire savings and all of his material possessions, along with the family home, had been confiscated, but it was not enough. The final fall of the magistrate's gavel yoked Gregory with the debt and sent him to labor on Trenton's farm where it would take several lifetimes to pay off his father's folly. Gregory rolled his shoulders as if he could feel the physical weight of what was owed to Trenton.

He skipped a few of the rocks in his hand across the pool in quick succession and tried to let go of his hard feelings. There was nothing he could do besides keep his head down and try to stay out of trouble. Something he was already failing at, being out of the farm's boundaries and in this fairytale grotto.

Gregory's mind wandered to the idea that it was strange no one else seemed to know this place existed. It was nestled in the woods beyond Trenton's fields, its waters feeding their crops, but it was never mentioned. As he considered asking some of the other farmhands about this place, the thought fluttered away like a butterfly, and he returned to watching the ripples of his skipped stones expand and then fade into the surface of the water.

The sun set, and fireflies emerged to do their twinkling dance in the twilight. Relaxed, but drained from the day, Gregory set off to find his bed.

When the next day bloomed in fiery oranges, pinks, and reds, Gregory splashed water from the horse trough onto his face, washing away the last vestiges of sleep. He had dreamed of her again last night, as he had done every night since arriving on the farm. But, the harder he tried to recall details of the dream, the quicker it evaporated into nothing other than a lingering feeling of loneliness.

"Oi! Boyo!" a gruff and gravelly voice called from behind him. Gregory stiffened. Turning, he inclined his head politely at the beast of a man that lumbered toward him. "Stop yer lollygagging and get to work. I don't pay you to smell the roses."

Gregory accepted the spade that was shoved at his chest and swallowed a retort about the lack of roses as well as wages. While it was true that Trenton paid the workers on his farm, he also charged them for tools, lodging, food, clothes, and anything else he could think of. In the end, as with most places of employment in the barely tamed countryside, the workers ended up drowning in debt, such that there was little hope of freedom. His expenses plus his father's debt would indenture his family line for many generations, for Gregory had no doubt that whoever held ownership of the debt when he died would seek out his next of kin, his sisters, and their families to pay what he could not.

"A fox got into the hen house last night. Clean it up," Trenton barked, and before moving on, he grabbed Gregory's arm, pulling him up onto his toes and bringing him to eye level. "I've already charged the slacker responsible for not latching the gate properly for the loss of my property. Find the fox and kill it, or everything else it destroys will be added to your debt." Trenton released Gregory with a shove.

"Yes, sir," Gregory said with as much deference as he could, not wanting to give the farm baron any more excuses to add to his insurmountable sum. Trenton stalked off, barking at other workers, and Gregory sighed with relief.

It was a short-lived reprieve, for behind the oppressive taskmaster flounced his daughter, her gait such that all the lace and ruffles of her fine clothes bounced. Other workers paused to admire the effect as she passed, but Gregory stood still and lowered his head, hoping to avoid her notice. No luck.

She stopped next to him under the guise of adjusting her shoe, and the expensive fragrance she wore wafted over him, sweet and peppery. Looking up at him through her long, dark lashes she purred, "Hello, Gregory, darling. Did you miss me?"

Keeping his eyes forward, he replied evenly, "Hello, Juliette. Did you have a nice time in the city?"

"I got a new dress. Like it?" she said, twirling with devious grace.

“It’s nice,” Gregory answered, his gaze still forward and a fervent wish pounding in his heart for her to go on her way.

A glare replaced her doe-eyed expression, a hint of the dragon that lay beneath the sugary veneer. “Nice? Fine. Be that way, Gregory. See if I care.” In an instant, her vapid expression reappeared, and she resumed her sashay down the lane, following her father. Gregory shivered. He had made the mistake of falling for her charms once, and it had nearly cost him his life. Rubbing the scar on his neck, he headed in the opposite direction to start the grizzly work he had been assigned.

2

Introductions

Celeste waited with bated breath to catch sight of him, and she was rewarded once again as he entered the glade, the sinking sun illuminating his arrival. It had been so long since she had seen another person, and now, she had been blessed by his visits for months. He, of course, knew nothing of her, as she had yet to show herself. There was a simple joy to his presence here that she did not want to interrupt.

He carried with him a squirmy sack, and Celeste frowned, watching from the waterfall. Her visitor gingerly set down the bag and untied it, springing back as a blur of red shot out and darted into the underbrush. Celeste could feel the creature's panic and confusion.

"Just don't tell anyone," the young, rumpled, and dirt-stained man said, calling after the fox, "and don't eat any more of Baske's chickens, please." He turned, giving Celeste a better view of the tired frown darkening his countenance. "I've got enough of other people's burdens to deal with," he said flatly.

He picked up a handful of smooth stones and began to skip them across the pool. Celeste almost giggled at the sound they made as they hopped across the water. Such a silly thing, to be so happy to have another soul near her and yet not have anything to do with him other than watch his nightly ritual.

Her delight at his presence turned to a frown of her own as the shifting sun highlighted his clothes hanging more loosely on him than they had before, and exhaustion being more deeply set into his features. Concern pulled her to the edge of the watery curtain concealing her.

“Why’d you have to go and do this to me?” he growled as he flung his next stone as far as he could. It splashed into the shallows on the far side of the pool. Celeste retreated further into the waterfall. This outburst did not match his usual contemplative posture. He threw the rest of the rocks with a wordless shout, and they splashed into the water, their ripples discordant. Sitting down, he pulled his knees to his chest and rested his head on them. After a moment, Celeste ventured closer to the edge of the cascading water once again. She had not been interested in leaving its boundaries in centuries, but now, she was tempted, drawn to this mysterious man.

He sat at the edge of the water and heaved a sigh, then threw himself back, his arms and legs spread wide as he released some of his tension and relaxed into the soft, loamy grass. Softly he said, “I wish...” Centuries-old magic stirred, and Celeste pushed on the edge of the water, ready to obey the mystical mandate that his words awakened. The water resisted her intention to make a simple introduction and held her firmly within itself. Sighing, she abided by the rules of her confinement, set forth nearly two thousand years ago.

She closed her eyes as she prepared to manifest herself, her curse requiring more theatrics than she cared for.

The surface of the pool began to ripple, then bubbled as she effused her essence into the water. A stream of bubbles and water rose from the middle of the pool's surface. Celeste's visitor sat up, his mouth hanging open as he watched her coalesce in front of him. Her body, comprised of water and bubbles, and her once dark, flowing hair, now colorless, reflected the greens and browns of the flora around them. She gave him a small smirk. While she disliked the way she was forced to interact with others, their reactions of awe and surprise when they first saw her always proved amusing.

The man fell forward on his hands and knees and crawled closer to the edge of the water. Scrambling to his feet, he waded into the water until it was up to his knees, unable to come closer for the steep drop of the shelf on which he stood. Celeste, her smirk fading and an uncertain feeling building in her core, scanned his face. It seemed familiar. His eyes were wide with recognition as well. "It's you," he said softly.

"Not the response I usually get." Her reply came out with an effervescent distortion.

He smiled, "You sound like what I imagine a babbling brook would, if it were to speak."

Celeste could not help but return his smile.

"I've seen you in my dreams. Dreams that usually slip away, no matter how hard I try to hold on to them. Nevertheless, seeing you here, they've come back with solidity. In my dreams, you are more human than water, but it is you." He started to take another step forward.

"Don't," she said, holding up a hand, instructing the water to push him back. The current she summoned gently escorted him back to shore. The sun had begun its journey to slumber, and its brilliance refracted in her arm, lending her its colors. "You should go, before it grows too late. Rest well, and mayhap we will speak in your dreams tonight." Celeste summoned her will into the palm of her hand, and it sparkled and twinkled with power. She brought her hand to her lips and softly blew, the glittering manifestation riding the breeze and descending upon him. He blinked, and she was gone, tucked back into the waterfall behind him. She watched as he followed her magic enhanced suggestion and left the glade to find his bed.

Celeste called to the fox that he had released earlier, and it poked its head out of a bush on the other side of the pool. "Come," she beckoned, adding some mystical encouragement to her words. The young tod gracefully obeyed, coming to sit where the man had been, her magic overruling its urge to run away from his scent.

Summoning a sparkling trout into the shallows, she gently said "You are safe here, little one, and will not go hungry." She settled into a cross-legged position as the fox watched the fish swim away. "Now, tell me what brings you here." He looked at her, and she gathered flashes of hunger, flying feathers, a nap in a cool den, and sudden capture. Panic and confusion, then freedom.

"Interesting," she said to herself, turning to look towards the entrance of the hollow. She extended her senses and followed the brightness of the man's soul as he got farther from the waterfall and wondered what it could mean.

3

Well Met

Gregory was sweaty and covered in more grime than usual, but he did not care. He did not even care that his mood was contrary to his misfortunes that morning. His pants had been wet when he put them on—only adding to the conundrum of his missing memories. Then, after visiting the slop house Trenton called a dining hall, three of the other farmhands had accosted him, their leader on a mission to teach him a lesson for offending Juliette the previous day. He had punctuated his lecture on manners with solid blows to Gregory's gut.

Afterward, as he lay gasping for breath on the ground, he was informed that Juliette had given the goon the privilege of attending to her that day. He had vigorously relayed with a kick that she wanted Gregory to assume his farm duties. He shook his head at the memory as he shoveled manure around fledgling pumpkin plants for that poor fool. Juliette's temperamental moods were more dangerous than her father's consistently sour one.

By all rights, he should have felt dour too. Nevertheless, he was buoyant—the source of his good mood a wonderful dream from last night that sat right beyond the grasp of his remembrance. Pushing away unpleasant recollections of the morning, he focused his mind on trying to grasp that dream. It danced just beyond his reach with a coy smirk.

The hours passed quickly, and he soon found himself finished with his work and hiking into the woods beyond the farm. A well-worn trail led him into the cool depths of the trees. It felt familiar, only he was sure he had never been here before. Birdsong invited him further, and soon he found himself at the entrance to an enchanting glade.

Its beauty stole his breath away. Soft meadow grass, dotted with flowers, led to the clearest pool of water he had ever seen. Through the reflection of the sky and fluffy white clouds, he could see to the bottom where minnows darted around reeds that swayed gently in a comforting breeze. Mist touched his face like the delicate trespassing of a thousand tiny butterfly feet, and his attention was brought to a waterfall that spilled down the other side of the hollow. There, standing in the flowing water that comprised her form, was a woman.

It was her. The one he had seen in his elusive dreams ever since coming to Trenton's farm. All of which were now solidified back into place, as well as memories of their meeting yesterday. Last night had been the first dream in which she had spoken to him, asking him to visit her again.

Without a thought, his feet moved him closer to where she stood watching him with amused eyes. He tried to climb to her, but the rocks were too slippery.

She smiled, and Gregory felt his heart would burst out of his chest. Other women who previously piqued his interest merely increased the pace at which it beat; never had they inspired the gymnastics it was currently attempting. The bubbles and currents that gave her shape swirled, and then she was gone. Gregory whipped his head around looking for her. He stepped back from the rocks and peered into the falls. A burbling giggle from behind pulled him around instantly to where she was standing in the middle of the pool, just as she had yesterday.

"Hello," she said. "I'm glad to see you again."

"Me too," Gregory agreed as he made his way to the water's edge and sat in the grass.

"What's your name?" she asked as she moved to sit in the shallows in front of him.

"Gregory. And yours?" She looked taken aback by his simple question. "It's only fair, don't you think, since you now know mine."

She glanced back at the waterfall for a long moment, then turned to meet his gaze. "I am Celeste."

"I am honored to meet you, Celeste." He inclined his head and made a flourish with his hands. She, in turn, bowed her head as well.

"Well met Gregory, well met."

His mind clearing somewhat from the euphoria of earlier, he asked, “How is this possible?” He waved his hand toward her, indicating her general form.

“Magic.” Her face was straight and her tone so matter of fact, it left him speechless for a moment.

Gregory leaned back on his elbows and looked into the sky. “I must have been given some bad slop at breakfast this morning, or Juliette’s goons must have hit me too hard. I’m hallucinating.” He patted up and down his body and felt his forehead. “No fever, and I feel intact, but still. Here I am talking to a figment of my imagination.”

A gush of water washed over them, knocking him onto his back. “If I am nothing more than your imagination, why then are you truly wet?” Her playful eyes twinkled in the setting sun.

“That’s a good question,” he said, standing and shaking water from himself. “I must have fallen into the water while in my delusional state.”

She laughed, and Gregory’s soul lit up. He glanced at the sun, hanging low in the sky. Bed checks would be soon. “I have to go.”

She nodded as the first hints of twilight lent its dusty colors to her form.

"Will I see you in my dreams tonight?"

"Mayhap," she said, grinning cheekily. Then, with a splash, she was gone.

Chuckling at the thought of talking to his imagination, Gregory left the glade feeling light. As he stepped from the tree line and back onto Trenton's farm, he was once again wondering at the source of his good mood. And why was he wet from head to toe?

4

Recollections

Celeste brought bubbles to dance on the surface of the shallows and delighted in watching the young tod hop in the funny way foxes do as he pounced on them. There were many animals in the glade, but this one was special; it had been brought to her, rescued, by him.

Two thousand years ago, she had been trapped in these waters, and a spell had been placed over the area. It was hidden from the minds and the memories of the world, save those who sought to bring tribute to the witch. They would bring their shiny tokens, chasing a whisper that an offering would grant their heart's desire. The witch would channel Celeste's imprisoned power, sometimes giving supplicants what they truly wanted, but often it was a twisted version that only brought the solicitor pain.

Then, blessedly, after a few centuries, the witch died, poisoned by her own descendant. A daughter four generations down the line had been taken under the guise of tutelage. The witch wanted another source of power, and when the girl learned she was to be more servant than pupil, she slipped deadly herbs into a cup of mulled wine. Her goal was to take the hag's power—and Celeste's—for herself. Thinking herself clever, the girl had slipped into the woods to wait for the witch to die.

Indeed, the witch went to bed with a stomachache and died in her sleep, but she was still able to twist one last wish, because the glade's bewitchment was a secret she took to the grave. It stole the knowledge of Celeste and the glade from the betrayer's memory the moment she left. For a few years, others who decided to test the rumors of the wish-granting witch in the woods found their way, and Celeste, compelled by the spell of her imprisonment, granted their wishes. She had the water carry their tokens into the cave behind the waterfall, piling them onto the others the witch had hoarded. A fortune of baubles and bits lay forgotten behind the cascading water, alongside the witch's dusty remains.

Many lonely centuries passed, and then a curious thing happened. Gregory appeared over the hill. He carried no treasure to be exchanged, no secret desire only magic could make manifest. No. He simply came to skip rocks on the pool of water at the base of the falls. Still more curious, he had known her from his dreams. His soul felt good to Celeste—honest and kind. She had tried to visit his dreams again last night, but he must have slumbered too deeply for dreams. No matter; she had hope he would visit her, just as he had every night without fail for many weeks.

The sun finished its descent, and twilight blanketed the sky. Gregory did not come.

Celeste sat on top of the water just in front of the falls. How curious that her ancient heart could break at his absence after such a short acquaintance.

The cooling night air brought forth a mist from the surface which reflected the light of the moon. An idea danced in those midnight vapors and tempted Celeste. She accepted its invitation and exhaled, joining her essence with the fog. It was still water of the falls; thus, the conditions of her imprisonment were satisfied. Conjuring a breeze, she pushed herself and the fog across the water toward the entrance of the glade where a stream pulled its water down the hill and into the forest. Gently, she guided the breeze, enough to propel her toward where she hoped to find Gregory but not so hard as to disperse the fog.

The technique was familiar. She recalled sneaking out of the glade in this manner during the early days of her curse. Even though considerable time had passed since she had experienced any desire to see outside her verdant prison, the technique still came easily.

Soon, the stream emptied into a canal that fed irrigation lines of a large farm. Fields stretched east and west into the night. How the world had changed while she was tucked away in the waterfall. All manner of tools and metal machinations she had never seen before littered the area. Beyond the fields lay large buildings. Celeste could sense the essences of many creatures and men.

Coalescing some of the fog into her womanly form, she walked on the water of the canals, careful to gather those parts of the stream that were from her waterfall and step only on those. She would not be able to go much farther, as water from other sources diluted hers, thus marking the edge of her prison. At the end of the canal she had been traveling, she stopped, unable to go forward. Most of the farm was asleep, animals in their pens and men in their long buildings. On the far side of these structures was a large, opulent house. She sensed fewer souls there, but none were Gregory.

Returning her focus to the long houses where many men slept, she searched more thoroughly for him. He was not there. Had he truly abandoned her?

When he was in the glade, he had behaved as if magic was gone from the world, but she saw fragments of the dream walkers—a rare people even in the days of her youth—woven into his soul. That was how her mind had found his dream the other night, just beyond the forest. It had been as a softly glowing beacon. All she sensed now was the dim buzzing of ordinary dreamers.

A group of people passed through an intersection directly in her line of sight, halfway between her and the fancy house. Celeste froze. One of the souls in the group was the golden goodness that was Gregory; another was one she had hoped to never sense again. It was not quite the same, but it bore the unmistakable twistedness of the malevolent soul who had cursed her all those years ago.

Celeste dispersed the fog and sank back into the water, commanding it to take her back to the safety of her forgotten glade. Maybe it was best Gregory had not come again. Hopefully the curse had stolen her from his mind completely and he would visit her no more. If he associated with someone that black of soul, Celeste wanted nothing to do with him.

5

Broken

Gregory nursed what he thought was a broken rib as he followed behind Juliette. She had found him after his day's work on his way into the woods and insisted on knowing what he was doing. He would have told her, if he had known himself, but the answers of where he was going and why eluded him. With Gregory unable to fulfill her command, she had her goons attempt to beat it out of him, but the assault failed to provide her with the answers she wanted.

Now, she marched down the main lane of the outbuildings toward the main house, her lackeys shoving him along. Dread threatened to dislodge the contents of his stomach.

Something prickled at the back of Gregory's neck, and he chanced a look around. An unseasonal fog hovered above the canal behind them. And was that a woman standing in the fog? No, *made* of fog? Gregory quickly turned away; he must have taken greater blows to the head than he thought. Yet the image of the foggy apparition triggered an ache in his heart and a regret for failing to visit the woods.

Boots stomping up stairs, followed by rough hands shoving him into the foyer of the farmhouse, brought Gregory back to his current predicament. In the space of a few ragged breaths, he found himself standing before Trenton, who sat at a large desk smoking a pipe while making marks in a ledger. "What's this, daughter?" he asked, not looking up from his task.

"I caught this farmhand trying to run away, Father," she said with a small deferential nod for Trenton and a devilish smirk for Gregory.

"I was n—"

A stiff punch to the jaw cut his protests short, and blood seeped from a new cut on Gregory's lip.

Trenton waved his hand. "None of that in here. I don't want blood on the rug." He looked up and sighed when he recognized Gregory. "You know, son, I usually don't take the time to get to know my workers, but yours is a special case. Not only did you come here as the liable party to a sizable debt, but you also keep doing things to add to that sum. You break tools, wantonly disregard rules, and now, you are trying to run away? Son, you're going to force my hand and make me drag your pretty little sisters into the debt."

"No!" Gregory struggled to break free of the hands holding him. "Leave them out of this."

Leaning back in his chair, Trenton set down his pipe. "What choice do you leave me? Your father's debt was large enough to take at least two or three generations to pay off. With the trouble you keep causing, it may take four or five now. Trying to run out on a debt you're responsible for is a serious offense there, boy."

Shaking out of the grip of Juliette's lackeys, Gregory tried to stand tall, but his injuries made him grit his teeth in pain and hold on to Trenton's desk for support.

"I wasn't running away; I was just going for a walk in the woods."

"Liar," Juliette hissed. "Father, it is well known that leaving the boundaries of the farm is off limits, and that our lands do not extend into the forest."

Trenton raised an eyebrow, inviting Gregory to respond, but all he could do was hang his head. It was true; he knew both the rule about leaving as well as where the farm's boundaries were. After a moment, Gregory said, "I've been going into the woods for weeks now, and I always come back."

"Really?" The evenness in Trenton's voice gave Gregory an uneasy, sinking feeling. "What is it you do there?"

Gregory grasped for memories floating just out of reach. All he could recall after his daily work was finished was walking into the woods right before sunset and walking out of them again soon after the sun had dipped below the horizon. Frustration threatened to boil over as his mind railed against the blank spaces where his memories of those evenings should have been. Never before had his dreams been missing, either, but ever since coming to the farm, his once clear and vivid dreams were gone, leaving only a sense of something missing in their place.

All he knew was that he felt peaceful and relaxed after both visiting the woods and dreaming. "I go to blow off steam. It's nothing. Certainly not worth all of this." He gestured to his bruised and bloodied body.

Trenton eyed him up and down, then cast a glance at his daughter, who crossed her arms and held her chin high. "I'm in a good mood, and despite your penchant for finding trouble, you've been a decent worker. I'll only charge you a curfew fine. However—listen to me carefully, son. If I have to speak to you again, I'll rustle up both of your sisters to start working down your debt."

Gregory started to protest, but Trenton cut him off with an upraised hand. His voice lost its evenness, taking on an edge that made Gregory feel cold inside. "Don't take my mercy for granted, boyo. I am perfectly within my rights to procure as many of my primary debtor's next of kin in order to have the debt paid off in as reasonable an amount of time as I see fit." With a nod, Trenton dismissed the group, putting his pipe back in his mouth and returning to his ledger.

Rough hands once again grabbed Gregory, dragging him from the room and out of the house. The goons threw him onto the cobblestones, adding scrapes to his hands and tearing a hole in his pants at the knee. While he lay there trying to catch his breath, Juliette knelt beside him and said softly, "I'm going to find out what you get up to in the woods, and you're going to be sorry you didn't tell me yourself."

Standing, she turned to go back into the house. As she did, Juliette ground her hard-soled boot onto his hand and gave a satisfied sneer when Gregory cried out in pain. Her cronies laughed as they left to find their own bunks for the night.

Slowly, painfully, Gregory stood and made his way to bed, nursing both his rib and his hand. Tomorrow's work would be beastly with his injuries.

A pit formed in his stomach that had nothing to do with the pain of each jarring step. There was no doubt in his mind that if Juliette found out what his missing memories were hiding, he would, indeed, be truly sorry.

6

Released

Celeste watched from within the waterfall as Gregory broke into the clearing. She had not bothered trying to find him in his dreams after seeing him with that dark soul last night. About to turn away and ignore his presence completely, she hesitated. Something about the way he carried himself caught her attention. He looked as if he could barely stand. When he made it to the edge of the pool, he dropped to his knees, breathing heavily and grasping at his side.

"Celeste," he said, panting. He turned his face toward the waterfall, bruising and swelling marring his visage, and called her again. "Celeste! I need to talk with you."

All the spite she felt from the night before evaporated, and she rushed through the water to where it met the grass on which he was kneeling. Manifesting her human-shaped form of bubbles and whirling eddies, she crouched before him and cried, "Oh, Gregory, you look awful! What happened?"

He chuckled, then winced before replying, "I feel pretty beat up." He gave her a slight smirk.

Celeste pursed her lips and reached out, gently grasping his head in her aqueous hands. They shimmered, and power infused water washed over him, seeking out and healing all his hurts. The cuts on his face closed, and bruises faded. He hissed as her magic found broken bones in his ribs and hand and knitted them back together. In a few moments, she removed her hands, leaving him dripping wet but whole.

His infectious smile spread from ear to ear, and he quipped, "I always end up wet when I visit here lately."

She laughed and sent a playful wave of water to wash over him. "Why, yes, it does seem to be the trend." Her humor faltered as she asked, "Gregory, what happened that you failed to visit me yesterday and arrived today in such sorry shape?"

Gregory sat back in the grass, worry painted on his face as he relayed the events of yesterday. Celeste listened carefully, asking an occasional clarifying question. The world beyond her glade was still a wicked one of violence and misery, the game for dominance over one another the same, just with different players.

Gregory leaned forward and asked, "Why can't I remember you or this place once I leave here? Why do I have dreams of you, but am also unable to remember them unless I'm here?"

Celeste shrugged and said, "Magic. I told you that the last time you were here. What? Why are you making that face? Don't tell me you have no magic where you come from."

"But we don't."

The idea of a world without magic was a hard one to comprehend. It took her a few moments before she was able to speak again. "Well, when I was young, magic was as much a part of the natural order as rain. And, just as some areas of the world have more rain than others, so too was it with magic and people. Some of us were born with more of the gift to use than others." Celeste's eyes glided over her beautiful prison, resting on the waterfall that concealed the source of her mystical binding behind it.

"You weren't always a magic water person?" Gregory teased, pulling her focus back to him.

She smiled back sadly. "No, sweet Gregory, no. Once I was flesh and blood. Young. Foolish and trusting." She told him of the greedy witch with the black and twisted soul that had trapped her there all those centuries ago.

He listened and nodded as she spoke, then gave his own sad smile. "We're both trapped then," he said, then went on to explain how his late father's debt had indentured him to Trenton's farm. "At least you've got a nice view and a fresh smell. My bunkhouse is next to the pig pens."

Celeste was shaking her head in commiseration when an idea bloomed in her mind. She stood suddenly. "If you had the means, could you buy your freedom, or must it be paid only by your blood and toil?"

Gregory scrunched up his eyebrows in confusion. "It can be paid off with money, goods, services, or labor. Though the only means I have are those of the strength in my arms and the youth of my back."

"Follow me," she said right before she dissolved into the water. Gregory stood and walked into the water, splashing around for a moment before he called out, "Celeste, my dear, I seem incapable of following you."

Celeste giggled as she leaned out from the waterfall. "Up here, Gregory." Dragging her fingers along the water, she parted it as if it were fabric and revealed a stairway made of boulders that led to a cave entrance. He sloshed over to the base of the falls and carefully navigated his way up the slippery steps. When he crested the top of his climb, his mouth fell open.

"Do you think this will be enough to free you from your oppressors?" Celeste asked with a hint of satisfaction.

Gregory stared at the piles of treasures that had been collected in those early centuries of her entrapment. Coins, precious stones, and jewelry overflowed from crates and chests. Magically preserved silks and fine clothes hung along the wall, though Celeste mused that those fashions would be less valuable now. Elegant furniture marked the living quarters of the long dead witch. Her bones lay on her bed where she had succumbed to the poison of her offspring. Crates with a thick layer of dust lined another wall, all that remained of the offerings of food. Bottles of once fine wines and spirits, surely turned to rancid vinegar by now, sat stacked neatly in a corner.

Gregory let out a low whistle.

"Well?" Celeste asked, amused at his amazement.

"This would free me several times over, Celeste. How ever did you come by such wealth?"

"They were tokens brought to the witch, given in exchange for her directing my powers to fulfill the supplicants' wishes as she saw fit. Even after she died, tributes were brought, and I was still bound by her enchantments to fulfill their desires. But, since I was free from her petty spitefulness, I was able to grant wishes in truth and goodness."

Celeste smiled to herself. She would grant his unspoken wish even if it meant she would likely be alone once again, forced to be forgotten. It was one of the witch's lingering cruelties. Knowing she would take solace in the certainty of his well-being, she said, "Take what you need and be free."

Gregory eagerly started to fill his pockets with trinkets of gold and silver. He reached for a particularly lovely silver diadem set with sparkling emeralds. Celeste recalled the heartbroken princess who came to exchange the headpiece and her title for a chance at love. She had been a sweet soul, but the witch, jealous of her goodness, had twisted her wish and forced Celeste to infuse her with a curse that turned her into a bird whenever the focus of her affections was near, never letting her find the happiness she sought.

Stopping short of the diadem, Gregory turned back to her, sadness in his eyes. "What of you?"

Celeste blinked. No one had ever asked of her wishes or well-being. He asked again, this time coming to the waterfall to stand in front of her. "Celeste, what will happen to you when I leave? Is there no way to free you, as well?"

Gratitude for his caring nature warmed her. "Don't worry about me," she said quietly as she gathered her will into her hand. "Go, take what you need. Don't come back. Live a peaceful life, and mayhap I'll see you in your dreams."

Before he could protest, she raised her hand to her lips and blew. The glittering power settled onto him, and he obeyed her compulsion, grabbing a few more handfuls of coins and jewelry. Then he left down the boulder steps and through the way he had come.

Celeste watched him leave the glade in the fading light. She sighed and settled into the waterfall, sorrow filling her core. Maybe she would sleep for a few centuries.

If she were made of flesh and blood, she would have cried herself into that slumber.

7

Shiny Dilemmas

Gregory woke with the crowing of the roosters. Dusty shafts of pre-dawn light drifted lazily through the ill-sealed slats of the longhouse, and more than a dozen men snored in straw stuffed cots, much like the one on which Gregory lay.

With sleep still clouding his thoughts, he wondered why he was still fully dressed in—once again—damp clothes and muddy shoes. This was becoming such a common occurrence that the mystery had faded into minor curiosity. Stretching, Gregory dismissed the dampness.

Things jingled and clinked around him as he moved. When he sat up, small objects fell off his ratty bunk and clattered to the floor.

Someone stirred a few cots over as the light streaming in through gaps caught on something glittery and threw golden reflections all around. Rubbing the rest of the sleep from his eyes, Gregory searched for the source of noise and light. His blood ran cold and his thoughts froze when he found it.

Covering his bed and the floor around it were more coins and jewels than he had ever seen before in one place, with more spilling from his pockets. Panic set in as his heart pounded in his ears and his lungs forgot how to breathe.

A groan and a creak from another sleeping laborer inspired action, and Gregory grabbed a traveling satchel from under his bed, quickly shoving the ridiculous amount of valuables into it. He filled it to the brim and firmly secured the clasps of the bag. Sweat beaded along his hairline as he stood, the weight of the bag and the mystery of its contents spurring his heart to beat faster than a frightened rabbit's. Where had this all come from?

A yawn sounded at the other end of the long bunkhouse, and more of the men he shared the space with started to stir. Gregory clutched the bag to his chest and hurried out of the building, jingling and clinking the whole way.

His only thought was to hide this mysterious wealth. Anyone who saw him with it would likely try to steal it, and he would wind up hurt or worse in the process.

Hurt? Gregory stopped in the middle of the street between the side of the long house and the pig pens, and he ran his hands over his chest. He was certain Juliette's goons had worked him over hard enough to bruise, if not break, some of his ribs. Bewildered, he checked his ribcage again. He was fine. A thought fluttered just beyond comprehension, and Gregory looked to the woods beyond the last of the fields. Maybe he could safely hide his new fortune there until he could decide what to do with it. No, something inside turned him away from the idea of going into the forest.

He looked down the street to where Trenton's mansion loomed. Thorny roses decorated the side of the house, right under the windows of Juliette's room.

Few dared venture over there, both to avoid the roses' bite as well as that of Trenton's temper for canoodling with his daughter.

Gregory ran as fast as he could while holding the jangling satchel to his chest. He grabbed a spade from one of the barns he passed, then spent the rest of the pre-dawn minutes fighting to get in the middle of the roses quietly and carefully. Impelled by the danger of his predicament and aided by his labor-enhanced physique, Gregory dug around one of the smaller back bushes, then leveraged it up by the roots. He nestled the bag with its glittering contents underneath before replacing the plant.

Standing back, he examined his work. The patch of thorny roses, with their delicate white blooms, showed no signs of disturbance. Gregory was covered with scratches on his hands and arms, while small tears decorated his shirt, but as he leaned on his spade, he heaved a sigh of relief.

His respite was short-lived as voices sounded from the room above. Something crashed, the tinkling of shattered porcelain echoing in the quiet of the early morning. Juliette screamed about someone's incompetence. Gregory ran as fast as he could to the fields, throwing himself into the first task that came to mind. He pulled at the weeds surrounding the young pumpkin sprouts with vigor, having no desire to add Juliette to his list of woes.

8

Bound by Blood

It had been days since Celeste sent Gregory away with the means to free himself. She had felt his dream-walking but had deflected him away, not wanting to chance breaking her enchanted command to leave his bonds behind and move on with his life.

She lay at the bottom of the pool, watching the sun move across the sky through the blurred lens of the water. Dragonflies buzzed and flitted across the surface. The day was idyllic, but still she felt empty. She was passing the time by slowly blowing large bubbles and watching them wobble to the surface when she felt a presence enter the glade.

Celeste grumbled to herself. She just wanted whoever it was to go away. Still, it was peculiar that after so many centuries of solitude to have not only Gregory visit, but another soul as well.

Grudgingly giving into her inquisitive nature, she drifted back to the waterfall, and the familiarity and darkness of the presence overwhelmed her. Celeste zipped into the falls, disbelief and fear flooding into her. When she saw who it was, she wanted to sink into oblivion.

Standing at the edge of the pool was a young woman in fancy clothes, her dark hair pinned up in intricate curls. The angle of her cheek bones, the tilt of the tip of her nose, and the shape of her mouth hinted at a familiar face from long ago. Yet it was her soul, twisted and dark and cruel, that blazed out at Celeste. The magic binding her stirred, and though she tried to resist it, she knew it was futile.

The descendant of the witch stood with her hands on her hips and surveyed the area. The beauty of the glade evidently lost on her as she twisted her mouth into a sneer. “What is so special about this place?” she huffed.

That was all it took. The magic practically threw Celeste out of the waterfall and pushed her up from the water. She stood on top of the crystal-clear pool, hands clasped before her and head bowed in submission. At first, the other woman was shocked, backing away quickly, but then she began to laugh.

“Who are you?” the dark-haired woman demanded after she had collected herself.

Celeste tried to stay her tongue, but the magic obeyed this distant connection to its source and words fell from her mouth. “I am Celeste.”

The woman pursed her lips. Celeste thought it made her look like a duck, but she could no more break a sneer through the demure servitude the original witch had demanded of her as she could speak unsolicited words.

“Well, that’s an odd name.” The descendant’s voice had a petulant, bored tone. She squinted and roved her gaze over Celeste’s form from head to watery toes. “*What* are you?”

Again, Celeste was compelled to answer. “I am the spirit of a powerful sorceress.”

The woman barked another laugh. "Under normal circumstances, I would think you to be foolish for saying such a thing, but it is hard to deny when it comes from the mouth of a girl made from water."

Celeste stared back impassively.

"Why do you linger, spirit?"

Bristling inside as the answer slipped off her tongue, Celeste replied, "I was bound here by a greedy witch. Supplicants brought her treasures, and in exchange she used my magic to twist their desires for her own entertainment."

The same selfish grin that had smeared the witch's face two millennia ago slid onto her heir's lips. "Oh? Do tell."

Celeste burned for this woman to leave, but she could do nothing except stand on the water and obey. While the sun moved through the sky, coming to touch the treetops with gentle golden hues, Celeste recounted the tragedies the witch had instigated. Finally, the descendent was satiated, and there was silence between them for a moment.

"So, they brought gifts, and the witch that captured you made you grant those wishes however she wanted. Now, I assume she didn't live forever, since she's not here cursing me, and I imagine it took a while for news of her death to get around." It was not a question, so Celeste remained silent, her neutral expression belying the screaming of her soul. The woman's eyes shone with greed and intelligence. "What happened to the gifts—the ones they brought after she died?"

"I put them with the rest." Celeste's burbly voice was even, but worry gnawed at her.

A glint in her eye confirmed this woman realized that Celeste had to answer to her. "Show me," she purred.

Celeste's skin would have crawled, had she any.

Dispersing into the water, she reformed in the middle of the falls. With a sweeping motion of her arm, she pulled aside the curtain of water, revealing the cavern entrance. The other woman quirked her eyebrow and gave a wicked smirk. All too soon, she had made the climb up the slippery rocks and stood staring at the piles of treasure the old witch had left behind. "So, this is where that fool Gregory has been spending his time. No wonder he held so hard to this secret."

Celeste ached to know what happened to Gregory but remained at the waterfall, watching in silence. The contrast between this woman and Gregory was as plain as the difference between night and day. Gregory had been full of wonder and curiosity when he saw the witch's horde, but this woman... Her eyes lit up with lust, and the air around her was thick with malice. She fingered the coins and the precious gems, then let out a groan of pleasure when she saw the bejeweled diadem of the sad young princess. After caressing it briefly, she snatched it up, putting it atop her head. "Ahh, that just feels right. What do you think?" she asked as she turned to face Celeste.

"It is a lovely piece with a sad story," Celeste replied.

Waving her response away, the other woman wandered around the rest of the cavern, stopping at the foot of the witch's bed. She stood a moment contemplating the remains. "How exactly was this hag able to capture you if you are such a powerful sorceress?"

"Blood magic."

"Interesting. Tell me more."

"She mixed my blood and hers with water from the falls. I don't know the exact spell she used; my magic is more elemental, more connected to the fundamental energies of creation. All I remember was soul-searing pain as she ripped my spirit from its mortal coil with a powerful spell that bound me to these waters and her will."

"And you never tried to escape?" she asked, eyeing Celeste with callous calculation.

Celeste reached out of the water and tried to pick up a coin from a nearby crate, but her watery hand dispersed around it. She shrugged and said, "I'm made of water; my ability to interact with the world is limited."

"But you didn't try to use your magic against her?" The woman turned back to regard the witch's bones.

Softly, Celeste said, "She told me not to."

The woman looked over her shoulder with a knowing grin. "You're still here, and your magic still works, so whatever she did to you did not die with her." She leaned over the bones and moved the blankets. They turned to dust at her touch, exposing the rest of the skeleton and the thing Celeste dreaded most about this woman's presence here. Around the remains of the witch's neck was a totem, untouched by time. It was still just as whole and vibrant as when Celeste had first seen it two thousand years ago.

Smokey, soot-colored quartz dully reflected the dim light that filtered into the cavern. Inside swirled the mixture of her stolen blood, the witch's blood, and the ancient water. It easily fit into the other woman's palm, and the gentle swirl increased to a maelstrom at her touch. Celeste's binding tightened as the totem accepted the witch's heir as its new master. The descendent beamed with malice as she looked up at Celeste, no doubt having felt the connection to the trapped sorceress's power.

Celeste steeled herself for the new reign of misery that was about to begin.

9

Thwarted

Gregory leaned on his pitchfork and wiped sweat from his brow. He took note of his enjoyment of the vigor of the hard work, the sounds of the animals, and watching the crops sprout and grow. When he first arrived on the farm, he had resented his entire circumstance. Aside from Trenton beating the possibility for joy out of his laborers, the confinement here due to Gregory's owed debt soured the potential beauty of this life. That would change soon.

For the last three days, while the farm duties kept Gregory's body busy, the satchel almost bursting with wealth buried under Juliette's window occupied his mind. He estimated that there was more than enough to pay off his debt. Maybe when he returned home he would put in a small garden and keep a few chickens, bringing what he had learned on the farm to reap benefits for himself rather than others.

All he had to do now was figure out how to apply the funds to his balance without Trenton and the magistrates suspecting fraud or theft. If Gregory had not touched the gold and jewels himself, he would be suspicious of their validity, himself. Even so, their appearance in his life left him flabbergasted.

The sun beat down on him, and the smells of the warmed pig pen assaulted his nose while big hogs rooted around in the freshly laid hay. Though still lost in the problem of getting the payment to the magistrate, he resumed spreading the hay around the space. When he turned to refill his pitchfork, Gregory saw Juliette sauntering down the lane, her eyes locked on him. Her expression was particularly triumphant, and it worried him.

An odd, dark crystal necklace lay in contrast amongst her ruffles and frills, and the hem of her skirt was damp and muddy. She carried an ancient-looking wooden pail.

As she drew nearer, the memories he knew were there just out of reach inched closer to his grasp. Juliette stopped in front of him with a grin that made his heart sink to the very depths of his stomach.

"Go get cleaned up, then meet me in the drawing room," she said as she hefted her bucket, adjusting it to afford herself a better grip, and then continued on her way.

Something about the pail and its contents pulled at Gregory. He dropped his pitchfork and ran to the bunkhouse, quickly changing from his filthy work clothes into the plain city clothes he had worn upon his arrival several months ago. Leaving his dirty clothes on the floor where he had dropped them, he ran to the closest irrigation canal and scrubbed his face, hands, and forearms. Something about the way he felt when that bucket was near fed his sense of urgency more than Juliette's command.

Moments later, he was at the steps of the mansion, sucking in air with ragged breaths. He had sprinted the whole way, desperate for unknown reasons. A butler let him in and showed him to the drawing room, closing the door behind him with an ominous click and leaving Gregory alone with Juliette. She sat in clean clothes in an overstuffed chair, fingering the strange grey crystal. It seemed to contain smoke that shifted and swirled within itself. The bucket sat at her feet, filled with crystal clear water. "Lock the rest of the doors, Gregory," she said in a seemingly bored tone, but with a malicious glint in her eyes.

"Uhm." He didn't move, instead glancing hesitantly at the two other doors that led into the room.

Juliette kicked the bucket. "You. Lock the doors and pull the shades."

Thin tendrils rose from the bucket like steam, sparkling with internal light, then they burst, covering the room with a shimmering haze. The doors clicked as their locks fell into place, and the shades snapped down.

Memories whispered from hidden recesses of Gregory's mind as his gaze passed over the main door, the side doors, and the windows, all of which had obeyed Juliette's command.

She leaned over the bucket with a twisted smirk. "Come now, don't be shy. I *know* you've met my Gregory before. Show yourself."

The water in the bucket began to swirl and bubble, slowly rising and coalescing into the miniature form of a woman, which took on the refracted hues of the deep burgundy furniture and rich mahogany trimmings of the room.

Gregory fell to his knees in front of her as his memories all came crashing back. "Celeste," he whispered as he reached a hand toward her, tears pricking his eyes.

"See, I knew you two had met, and, by the looks of it, you may be more than mere acquaintances." Juliette kicked the bucket to the side, sloshing water over the sides and eliciting a gasp from Celeste, who fell to her knees from the abrupt displacement. Juliette stood, towering over Gregory. "It doesn't matter. She's mine now and has to do whatever I say."

Gregory looked from Juliette to Celeste in question, but Celeste only bowed her head, sorrow written plainly across her watery features. "Oh, Celeste," he said as he tried to move closer to the bucket. Juliette side-stepped, blocking his path. She gripped the hazy stone hanging from her neck, and Celeste flinched.

"Make him sit back down," Juliette ordered.

"I'm sorry, Gregory," Celeste whimpered in her burbly voice. Collecting into her hand what looked like tears falling from her eyes and down her cheeks, Celeste blew on them, and similar shimmering particles she had used on him before flew from her hand. They swirled around Gregory, lifting him up and sitting him back into his chair.

"Shut up! Don't you talk to him," Juliette hissed, whirling around to face the diminutive Celeste, who still knelt on top of the water in the bucket. Juliette picked up the bucket and moved to a side table, where she removed the topper from a crystal decanter and emptied its light amber contents into a large-leafed potted plant. She held the empty bottle toward Celeste and waggled it at her. "Get in," she ordered, her tone flat and dangerous. Celeste raised herself on a stream of bubbles and shrank further in size as she transferred her form and some of the water from the bucket into the decanter.

Gregory tried not to choke on the lump of fear that had formed in his throat. "What do you want, Juliette?" he asked, finally finding his voice again.

Juliette returned to her chair, setting the decanter with Celeste on the side table next to her. "I want what any girl wants: power, money, attention." She paused, her hungry eyes lingering on Gregory. "Love."

Gregory tensed. "Don't you have enough of that? You're the daughter of a powerful farm baron. Trenton gives you whatever you want, and the laborers fall over themselves to do your bidding. Even I fell for your charms when I first got here, and I almost died for it."

"Yes, well what can I say? Enough is never really quite enough." Juliette leaned over to the decanter. "He's a mess. Hardly fit to be in the same room with me in his current condition. Clean him up, and put him in something more suitable for being my betrothed."

Gregory could not get his mouth to work as the tiny form of Celeste looked at him in defeat. His heart ached for the centuries she had endured fulfilling the whims of a black-hearted witch, followed by even more centuries of isolation, and his stomach churned at the thought of her being at the mercy of Juliette's impulses and machinations.

Before he could find his voice to protest, glittering power bubbled up and out of the decanter and hit him in the chest. It enveloped him, and Gregory felt cleaner than he had in months. When the power faded away, he was wearing a crisp three-piece suit, the color reminding him of the deep green shadows of the glade. Shiny brass buttons embossed with three wavy lines went up the center of his vest, with a matching trio on each cuff of his coat. It fit him perfectly.

"Celeste, go back to the waterfall. Back to the safety of the enchantment so Juliette will forget."

Celeste lowered her eyes and gave no response to his pleading.

Juliette snorted a derisive laugh, a bold contrast to the finery she wore. "She can't. I have this." She grabbed the grey crystal that hung around her neck on a velvet rope and held it up for Gregory to see. The thing looked old and new at the same time. He glanced back at Celeste, her expression confirming that Juliette spoke the truth. As his eyes flitted between the two women and the necklace, an idea formed in Gregory's mind.

Tugging on the jacket and settling into his new clothes, he attempted a smile at Juliette. "Good."

"Good?" Juliette scowled. "You're happy I have the trollop in a bottle?"

Gregory's mouth ran dry, but he continued with his plan. Leaning forward in his chair he said, "Yes... She was controlling me." The words came out awkwardly, and he rested his hands on his knees to hide their clamminess. "Her magic is strong, but the curse over her recognized you as its true master. I'm assuming." He motioned to the stone Juliette had returned to her chest. The ample ruffles of her neckline cradling the pendant and its swirling inner glow.

"Yes, she tells me I'm a descendant of the witch who caught her in the first place, making me a rightful heir to this bauble." She smiled. "Come, my love, let's go tell Daddy of our betrothal and have the servants begin preparations for the wedding." Gregory swallowed hard but held out his elbow, and she accepted with a giggle as she patted and primped her curls in preparation for her grand announcement.

His heart raced. He had no intention of telling her father anything, let alone *that.* Trenton was not one to tolerate amorous intentions from the workforce toward his daughter.

Gregory began to escort Juliette from the room but stopped just in front of the door. "Wait, my love." He choked out the words. "The last time he caught you innocently in my arms, I ended up against a tree with a knife at my throat and our picnic scattered. He won't receive this news well if I'm but a simple, debt-burdened laborer."

Juliette rested her hands on his chest and traced the designs in the fine brocaded fabric. "You're right. We don't want Daddy to add any more scars or to ruin your pretty face." She returned to the side table and poured Celeste and her water into a nearby crystal bowl. "A pretty place for my pretty pet," she cooed.

Celeste settled into a seated position, back straight and face neutral, but eyes alert, watching Gregory. He winked at her while Juliette's back was to him, and a frown creased Celeste's serene features.

"Oh, don't pout," Juliette chided, as though the expression was for her. "I want you to erase Gregory's debt from the farm's ledger and the memories of him from everyone on the farm except for those of us in this room." She turned toward Gregory and purred, "I want you to remember what I've done for you here."

Celeste stood, pressing her hands together in front of her heart. A fog formed on top of her bowl, then spilled over the side. It quickly covered the table and dripped to the floor. Tendrils snaked and drifted around the furniture legs, then out of the room under the doors.

Juliette pushed up the closest shade to watch the fulfillment of her command. "Oh, this is going to be fun," she whispered.

Pale mist soon covered the grounds outside of the house, and, after a few minutes, the whole farm was covered in the silky magic. Gregory cast his gaze to Celeste, who was deep in concentration. Juliette let out a malevolent giggle, and dread filled Gregory as he wondered what else she could possibly be planning to do with Celeste's powers.

Dropping her hands to her sides, Celeste said, "It is done. No one outside of this room will remember Gregory, nor his debt."

The fog receded, returning the way it had come, back across the farm, over the house grounds, under the door, and back up to the bowl where it faded into nothingness. Juliette clapped her hands together and crossed back to the door where Gregory stood. She pressed against him and closed her eyes, puckering her lips for a kiss. Gregory had tasted those lips once before, in his naivety, and he wanted nothing to do with them ever again.

He ran his hands up her back, and she shivered in anticipation. When he reached her neck, instead of holding her head and bringing his lips to hers, he grabbed the velvet rope that held the blood totem and yanked it up over her head, pushing her away in the process. Gregory maneuvered away from her and put himself between Juliette and Celeste.

"You thief!" Juliette shrieked. "You liar!" She lunged at Gregory, her face contorting into a hate-filled snarl. "Give it back, and I'll have my father kill you quickly."

Easily keeping her at bay with his labor-enhanced muscles, he held the totem above his head, well out of Juliette's reach. "No," he said as he grabbed one of her flailing arms and shoved her into a chair.

Juliette looked like a bull about to charge. Big, angry breaths flared her nostrils. Her hair stuck out at odd angles as its pins tried to flee, and she gripped the arms of the chair so hard as to drain the blood from her hands.

"No, Juliette. You can't do this to Celeste. I won't let you." Gregory threw the totem to his feet and stomped on it, instantly shattering it into a fine dust.

Juliette screamed and threw herself to the floor, desperately trying to scoop up whatever was left. Gregory turned around to find Celeste sitting cross-legged on the bowl of water, a playful smile on her tiny face.

"Thank you," she said in her burbly voice, full of relief—music to Gregory's ears. She stood and stepped out into the air, shimmering as she shed her watery form. Before his eyes, she transformed into a full-sized woman with long, flowing raven locks, amber-tinted skin, and coppery eyes that Gregory could get lost in for the rest of his days.

"I'm free," Celeste breathed, her voice a sweet, rich timber. She crossed to him, her eyes coming level with his nose, and wrapped her arms around him. Accepting the embrace, he encircled her with his own arms and held her warm, supple body against his. He felt elated and whole in a way he had not ever experienced with any other woman.

An almost inhuman growl sounded behind Gregory, breaking the peaceful bliss of the moment. Celeste pulled away just enough to look around him at Juliette, and he followed her line of sight over his shoulder. Juliette held a dagger high above her head.

"That power was mine! You stole it from me. I'll kill you. I'll kill you both," she raved, spittle gathering at the corners of her mouth. "No one will know either of you were here."

Celeste held up a finger, and Juliette stopped mid-lunge. "Shhh," she said gently. "Sleep." The knife clattered from Juliette's hand as she crumpled to the floor. "Sleep for a fortnight, and when you wake, remember nothing of me or Gregory." Celeste rubbed her fingers together and a small breeze carried her manifested words, like sparkling grains of sand, over to settle on Juliette's prone form.

"She deserves worse than just to forget for all the pain she caused as well as for the misery she would have caused with access to your powers. Maybe life as a toad for a while would do her some good," Gregory said.

"Perhaps, but it brings me no joy to exact vengeance. Simply knowing she won't harm me—or you—anymore is enough."

With Gregory's arms still surrounding her, Celeste ran her hands along his arms and rested them on either

buried the satchel and retrieved it before leaving the farm, his heart hopeful and his soul free.

Reflections

Epilogue

Wrens trilled and chirped as Gregory skipped rocks across the surface of the pristine pool. The stones no longer travelled as far or hopped as many times as they once did. It had been fifty years since his first visit to this idyllic place. While the tranquil glade was no longer a secret—the enchantment on it broken when he had smashed the witch's blood totem all those years ago—the staff of his estate knew to leave him in peace while he conducted his evening ritual. Although, these days, a patient assistant waited just outside the trees to help him traverse the trail through the woods.

A butterfly flitted just out of reach of a scampering fox kit, and Gregory smiled at the youthful frolicking. A glint off the delicate wings made his breath catch, but it was gone before he could focus on it. Deciding the glitter he thought he saw was just his old eyes playing tricks on him, he sighed. As he threw the last rock in his hand, Gregory mentally said goodbye to the place that had been his solace during those first days being indentured on the farm and then his place of respite as he moved from a laborer to a baron in his own right, boosted to the position by Celeste's generous gift. Something was telling him this was his last visit to this place.

Gregory emerged from the woods, leaning heavily on his assistant, just as the sun began to set, casting the old farm in warm golden hues. Trenton had spent a fortune trying to wake Juliette from her magic-induced sleep, leveraging all he had, including the farm, but to no avail. Most of his wealth was tied up in debts he held over the heads of his indentured workforce. Juliette woke at the end of Celeste's fortnight enchantment with no recollection of Gregory, Celeste, or the malice she had intended to wreak with her ancestor's pendent.

A small chuckle escaped him as he recalled the surreal feeling of their lack of recognition the day he returned to the farm to buy it and a large number of Trenton's debt holdings. He pardoned some debtors and made it easier for others to pay back what they owed. Over the years, the farm had also served as a base for several philanthropic endeavors, though currently it was functioning as a home for orphaned boys.

Boys who whooped at the sight of him emerging from the woods. Gregory chuckled and dug into his pockets as the younger ones ran over to him, handing each one a sweet. He ruffled their hair and sent them to wash up. The boys ranged from very young—still in swaddling—to strapping young men almost ready to set off on their own. Some came back and earned permanent positions as managers, caretakers, or laborers, while others went off to thrive in different industries. A handful were never heard from again after they left the farm. Such was the way of these things. Gregory tried to provide a stable and nurtured upbringing, but what they did with that was left to the boys.

On his way to the dining hall, Gregory reflected on the ups and downs of his life since Celeste released him from his indenturement. He had immediately reunited with his sisters and his mother. However, it was not until he showed them the grove with its hidden treasures and the ancient deed indicating him as the sole heir to a large parcel of land that they believed his story about a magical woman made of water setting him free.

Now, upon entering the boisterous room full of hungry boys, he thanked Celeste, once again, for providing the foundation for all he was able to do in his life. Especially for the ability for his mother to live out her remaining days in comfort, leaving her position as a washerwoman to become the governess of his home.

The day he found the decrepit manor house while exploring what Celeste had bequeathed him was a joyous one. Gregory had happily spent a few years restoring it, naming it Celestian House in honor of her.

His sisters had married good men and blessed Gregory with nieces and nephews, on which he doted. While Gregory found himself with a long-term companion from time to time, he never married. Still, his life was full, and he had done his best to live it well.

As was his weekly custom, he broke bread with the boys of the farm, enjoying their youthful exuberance, before having a carriage take him back to Celestian House. During the ride home, he mentally reviewed the provisions he had made for the boys' farm to be supported in perpetuity, as well as his other holdings. He felt at peace. All he had built would be taken care of when his earthly days were finished.

Stepping out of the carriage, he undid the top button of his shirt, feeling suddenly restricted. Gregory caught the worried glances the footman and his aide gave each other as his breath came more ragged than it should. He waved them off and took himself to his rooms, a large suite in the back corner of the grand house. He changed into his bedclothes, rubbing the discomfort that had formed in his arm.

Climbing into bed, he made a list in his mind of things that needed attending to the next day. Noticing the wheeze that now accompanied the tightness in his chest, he added calling on the physician to his list. Gregory closed his eyes, struggling to take a full breath as he felt himself slipping into slumber.

Then there was nothing. No aches. No pains. Nothing.

He opened his eyes to a brilliant whiteness, his bedroom gone. A beautiful blue butterfly flitted past, and a laugh tinkled behind him, one that filled his core with warmth and lightness. Then a voice sounded, sweet and rich.

"Hello, Gregory. Did you have a good life?"

Afterword

Thank you so much for taking the time to read *Celeste*. This story has been one of my favorites to write. It is also special to me because it is the one that set me down the path of writing the Novella Roulette series.

It all started as a game to play with my newsletter subscribers. They voted on a list of random words and the three winning words became the prompt for a story. Originally I wanted to keep them super quick and short, but each story got longer and longer. When the prompt for *Celeste*—pumpkin, complication, and waterfall—came in, the story that unfolded in my mind exceeded the length parameters. Instead of sacrificing the story for an arbitrary word count goal, I embraced it. This novelette was the result, and I loved it so much.

I've gone back and have been expanding the previous stories, so they can reach their full potential as well. Those will be Novella Roulette's #1-3.

I, also, collected and started on #5-8. They also start with a prompt of three random words, and the stories are emerging are so different. Some are fantasy, and some are sci-fi. There are also a variety of subgenres that are explored. The random roll-of-the-dice nature of these stories led to the whole collection being called Novella Roulette, because you'll never know what you'll get.

It's a fun and exciting way to write. The next story in the series is *Tiger Blessed* and it was inspired by the words truth, tiger, and decide. This fierce sci-fi features warriors, deception, some potential mysticism, and maybe some aliens...

Acknowledgements

This book would not be possible without the support of many people. First, my family whose love and excitement sustains me. Next, my writing group, without whom I would succumb to the pressures of my own self-doubt. My editors, Toni Suzuki and Angela Morse, along with my proof readers Myriah Hatch and Susan Isla, help me polish this story to make it the best that I can. Finally, my cover artist, Jessica Parker who brought a beautiful version of Celeste to life for the cover.

Also by Kay Melbrell

The Eternium Series

The Lost Spark

The Rising Spark (coming soon)

Epsilon: An Eternium Short Story

Novella Roulette

#1: Racer 38 (coming soon)

#2: Sprig (coming soon)

#3: The Peirce Memorandum (coming soon)

#4: Celeste

#5: Tiger Blessed (coming soon)

About the author

Kay Melbrell lives in a Houston suburb with her husband and their three young children. She spends most of her time doing mom stuff and writes stories when she can.

Want to get early access to upcoming Novella Roulette stories? Check out my Patreon.

Patrons get new early-access chapters sent straight to their email and have access to the entire archive. Check it out at www.patreon.com/kaymelbrellbooks

For new release updates, exclusive content, and more, sign up for my newsletter at www.kaymelbrell.com.